Boo to You!

PUMPKINS

Lois Ehlert

Beach Lane Books
New York London Toronto Sydney

That scary cat's back.
Boy, what a bummer!

PUMPKINS

Seeing
that puss
could spoil
our summer.

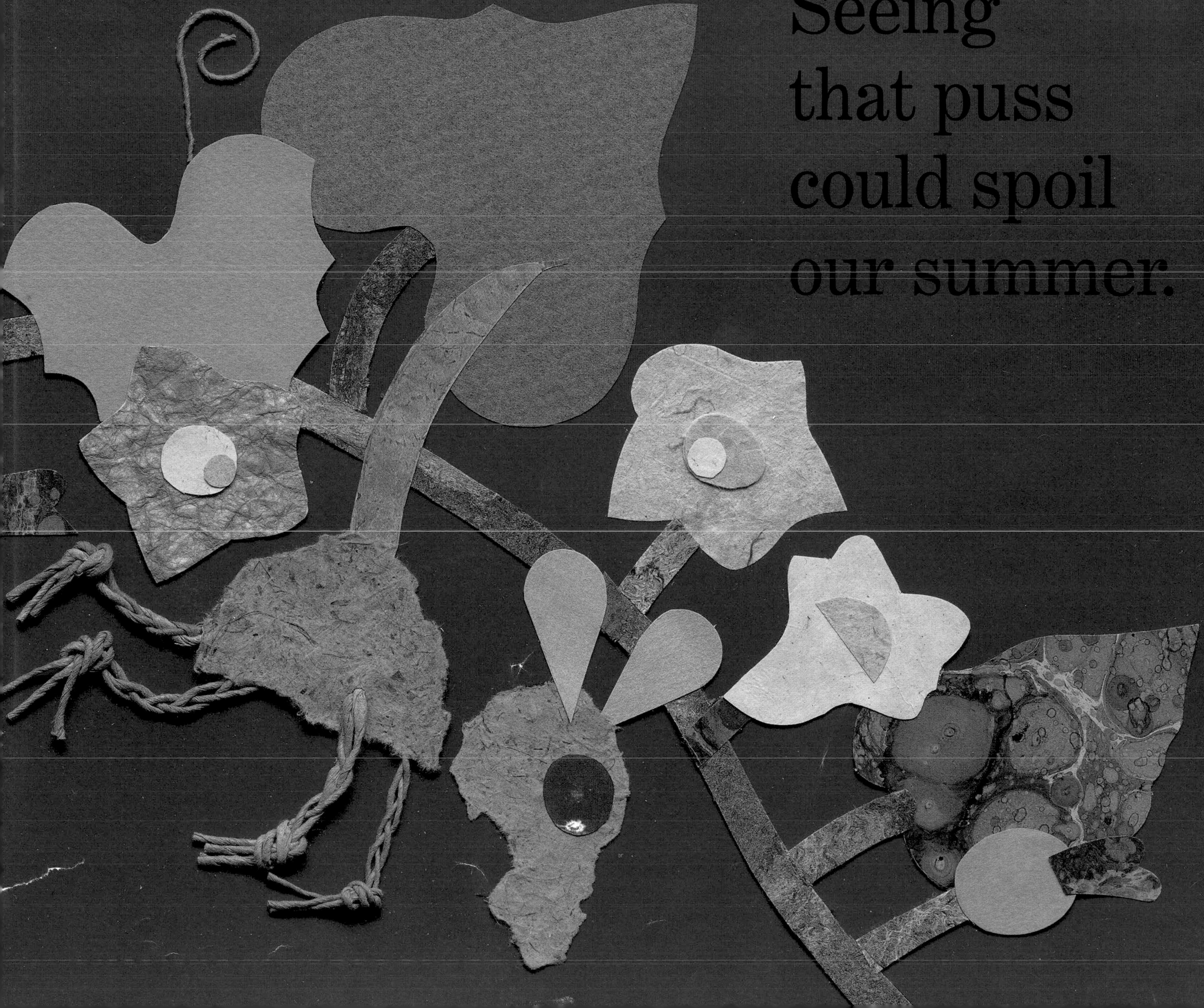

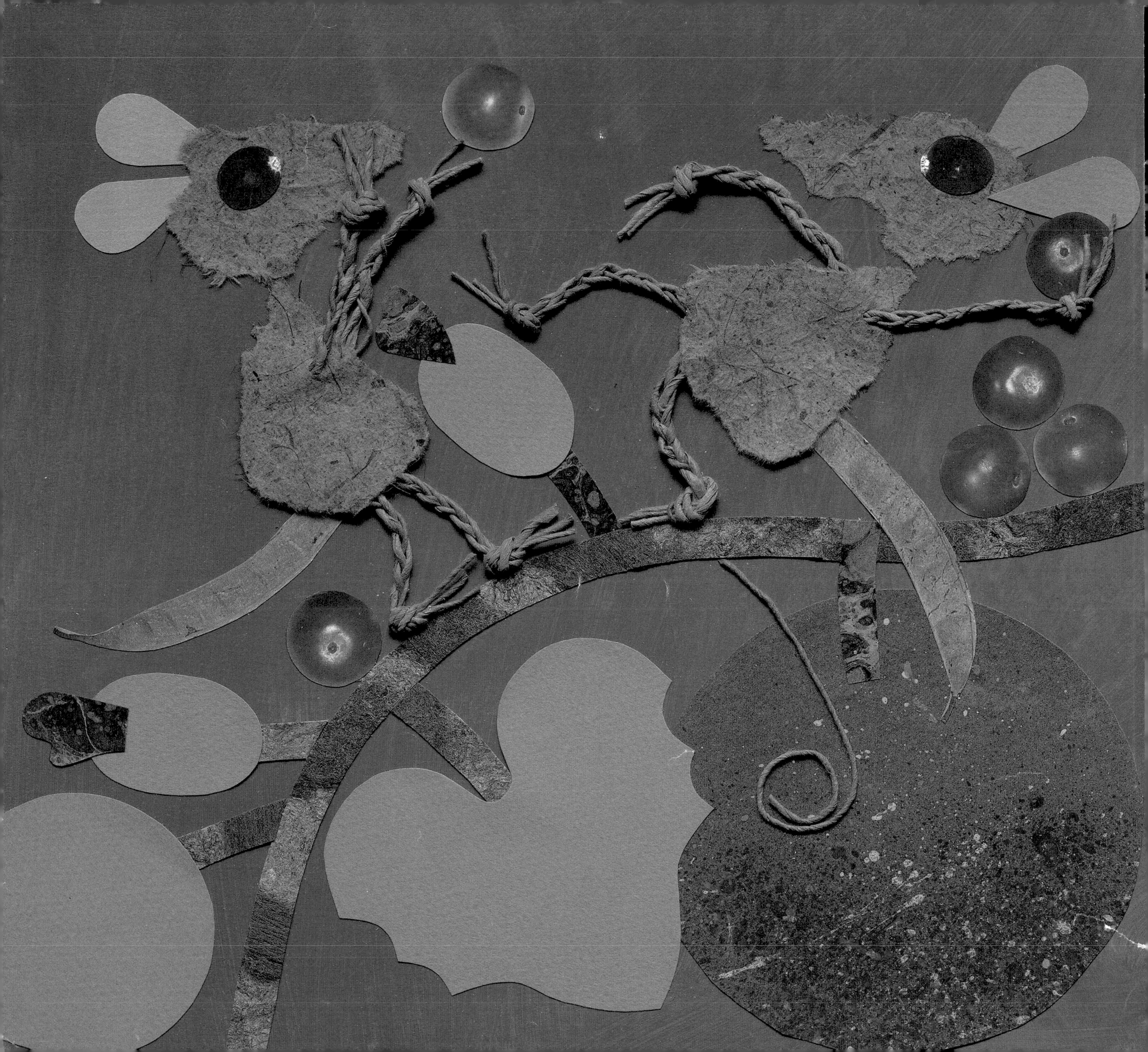

A raccoon or a squirrel might bite a veggie,

but a cat loves meat,
and that makes us edgy.

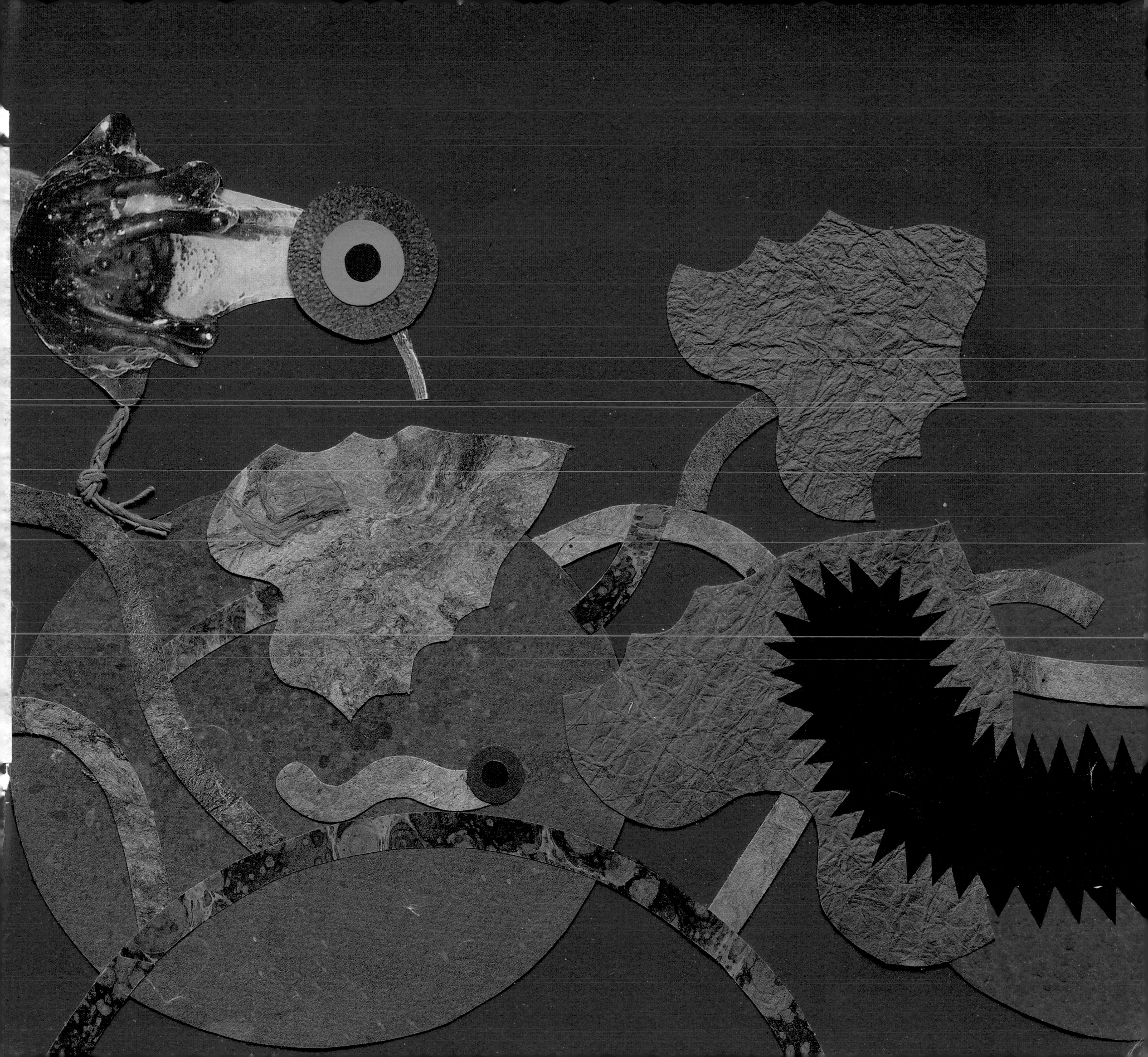

We're having a harvest party tonight.

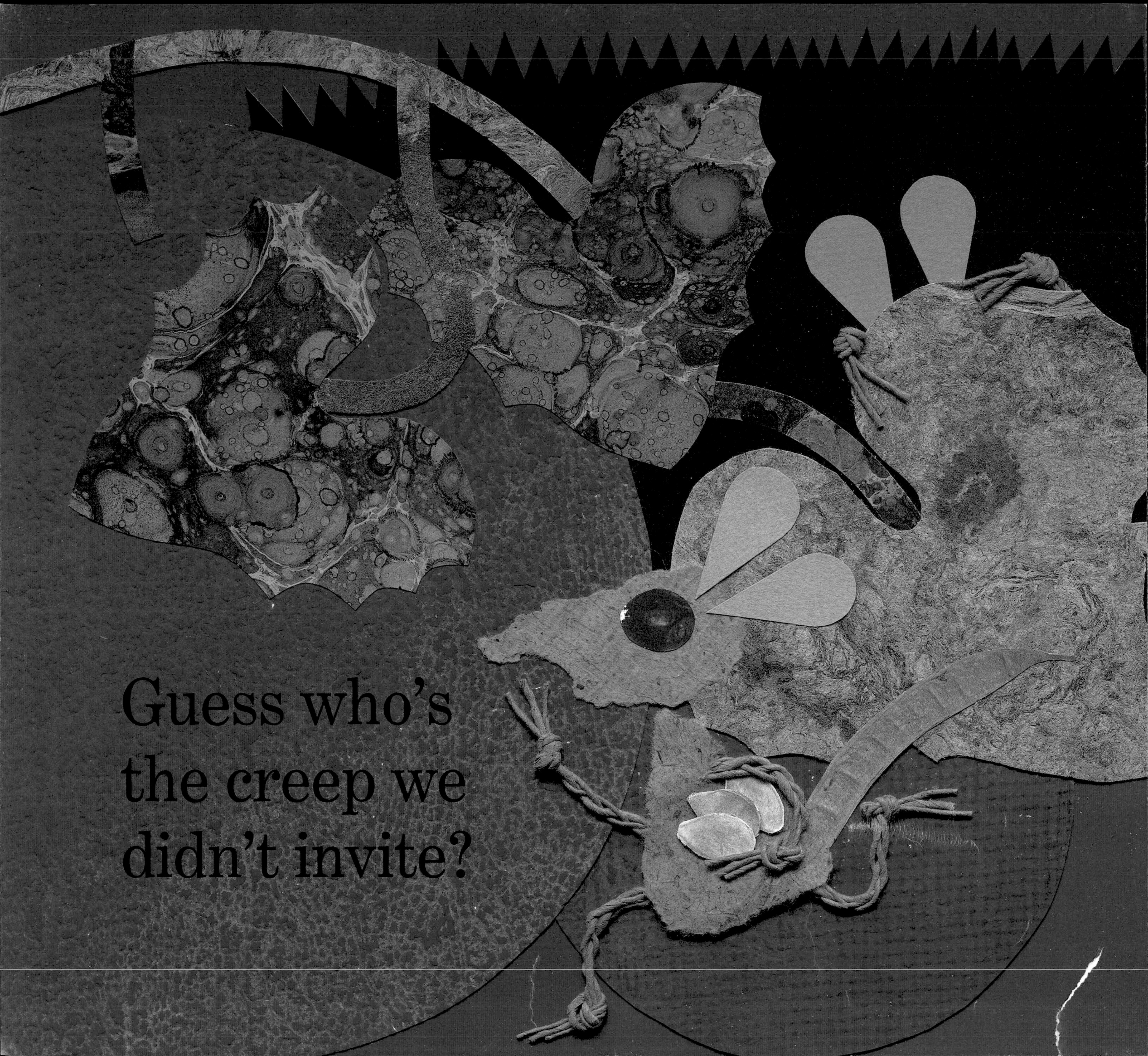

Guess who's
the creep we
didn't invite?

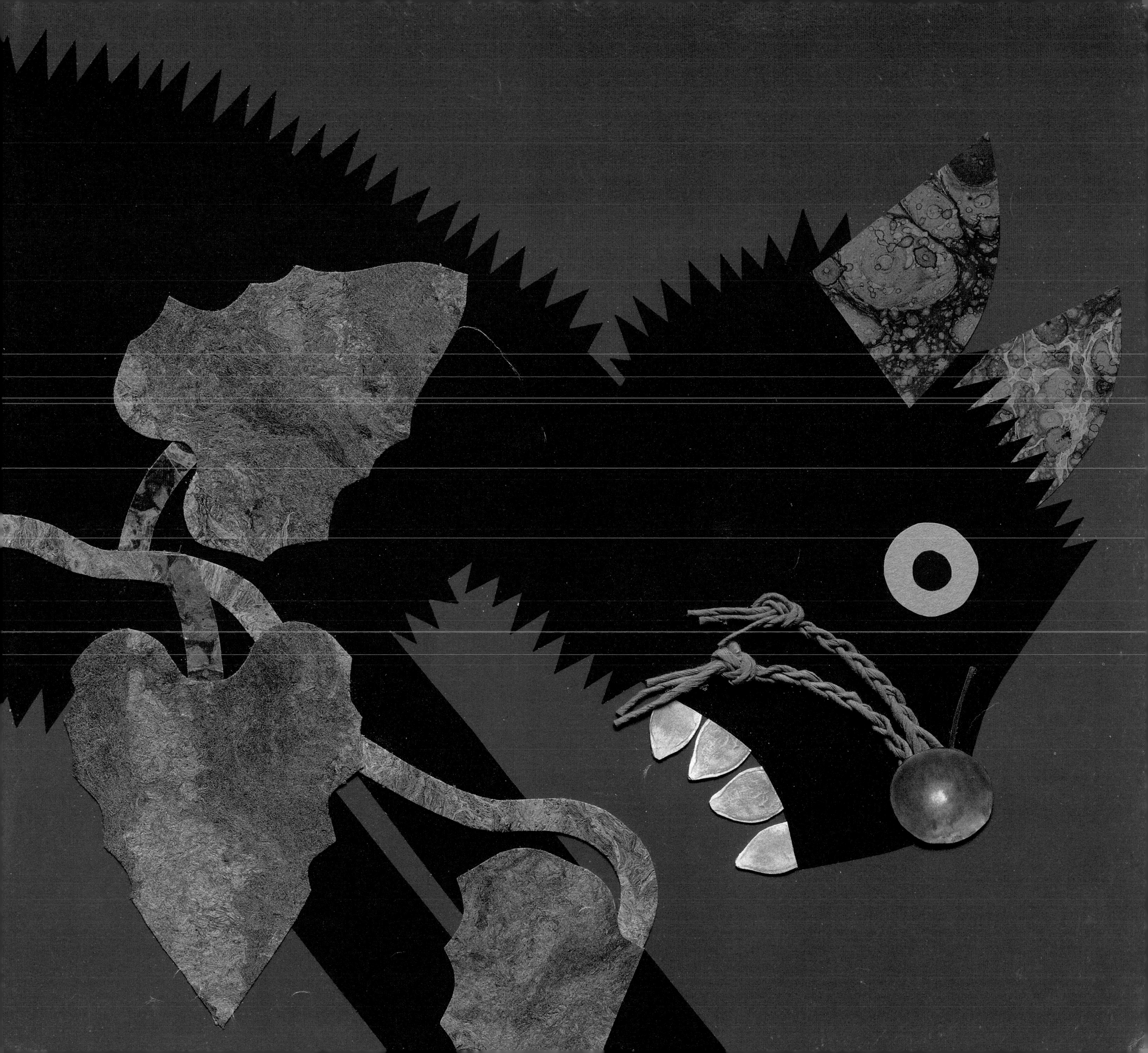

In the dark, these decorations sure look great.

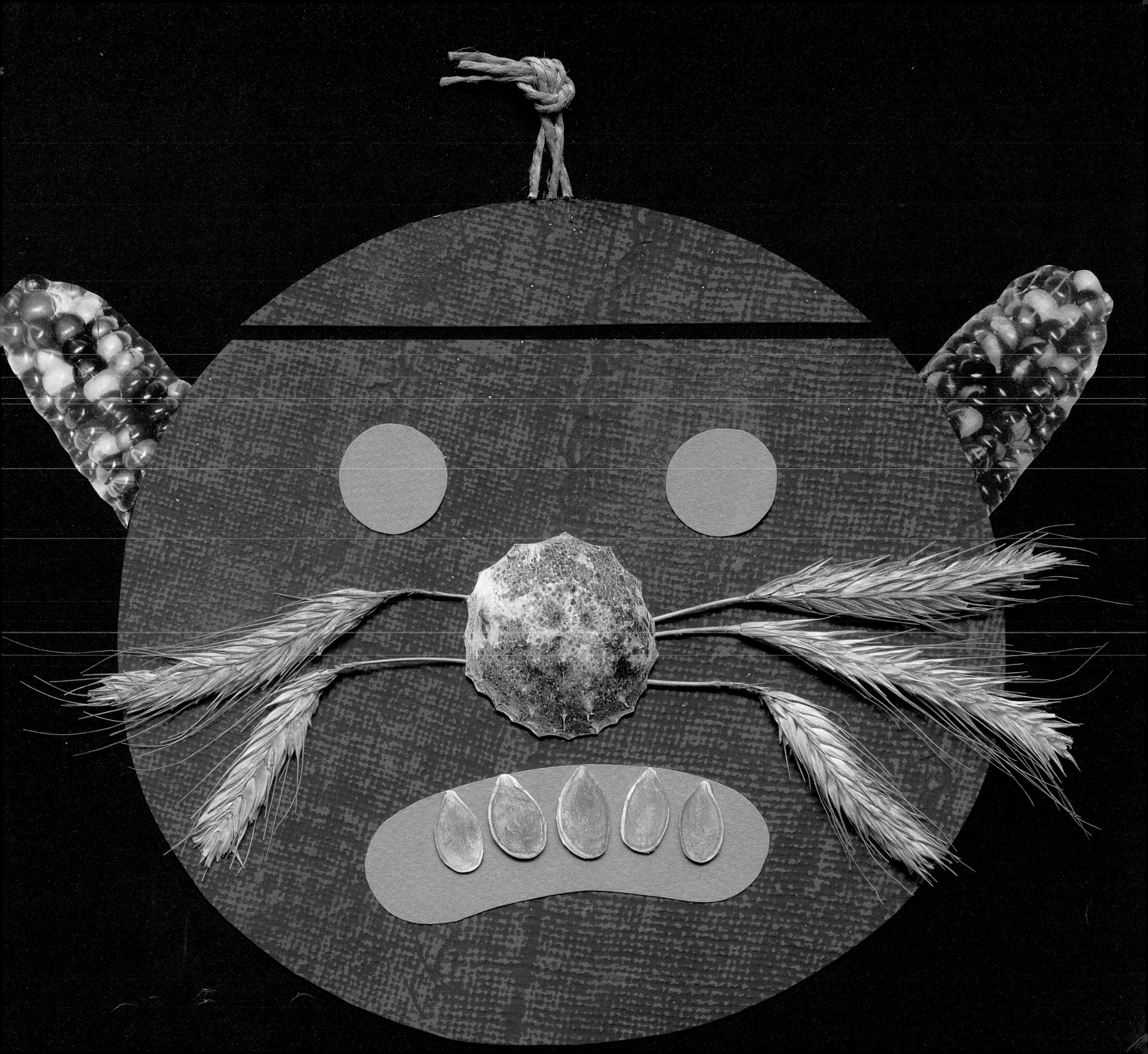

But we can't party yet.

We have
to wait.

Then the house lights flick off;
it's a spooky mood.

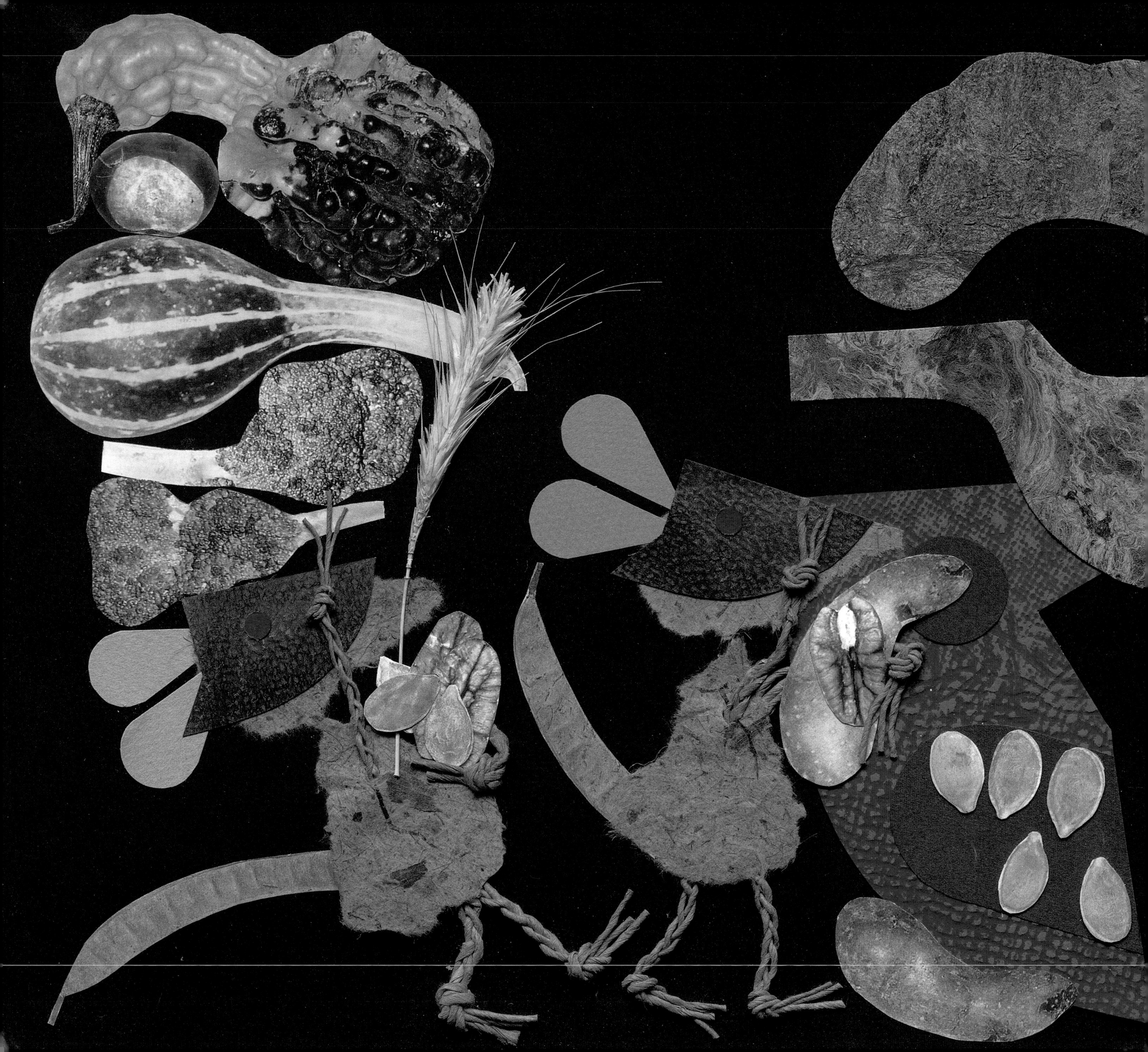

Let's put on our masks
and harvest some food!

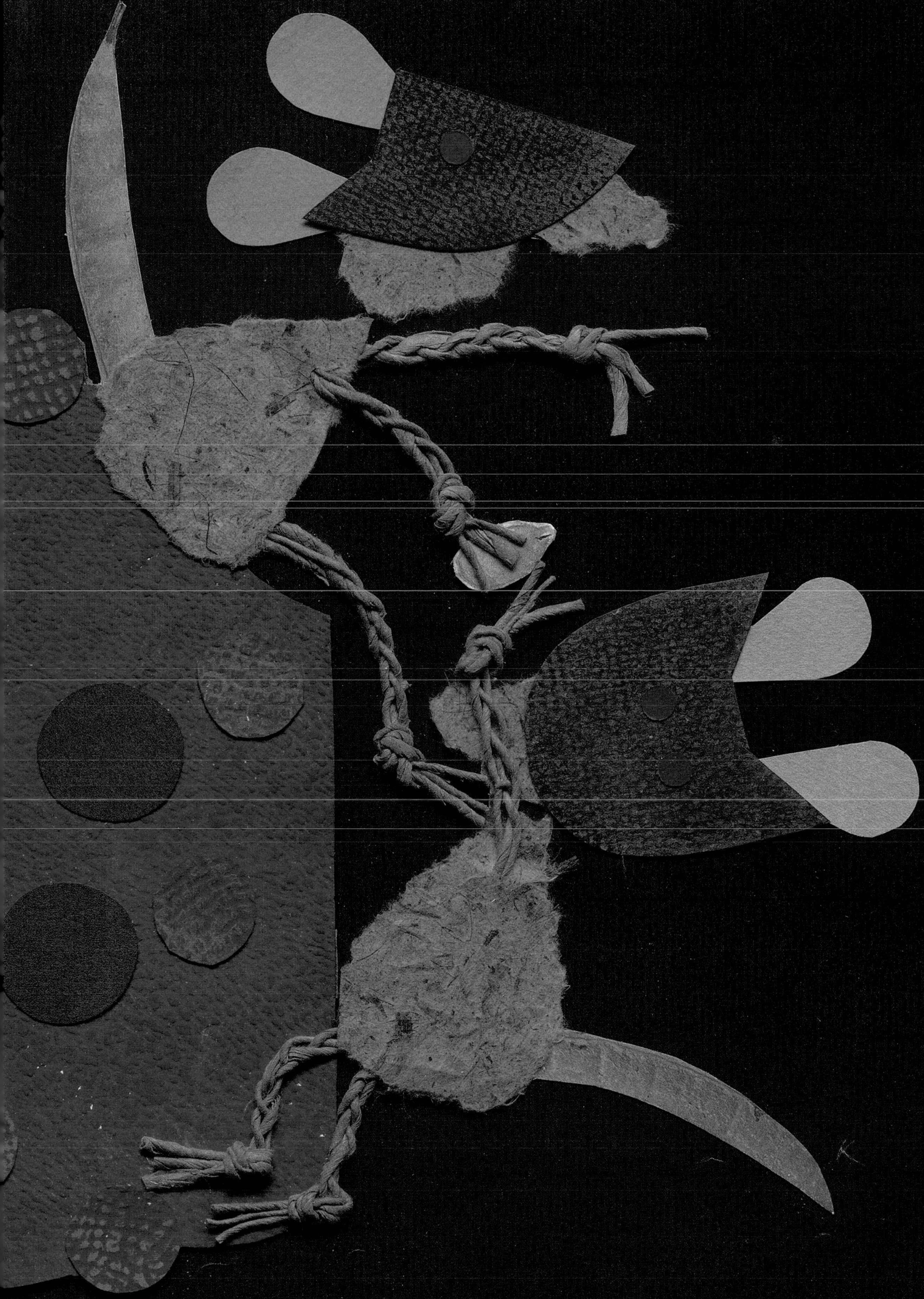

Just as
we're about
to dine,
that cat
peeks out
from behind
a vine.

But we know
exactly what
to do.

We'll *scare*
that scary
cat . . .

Boo to you!

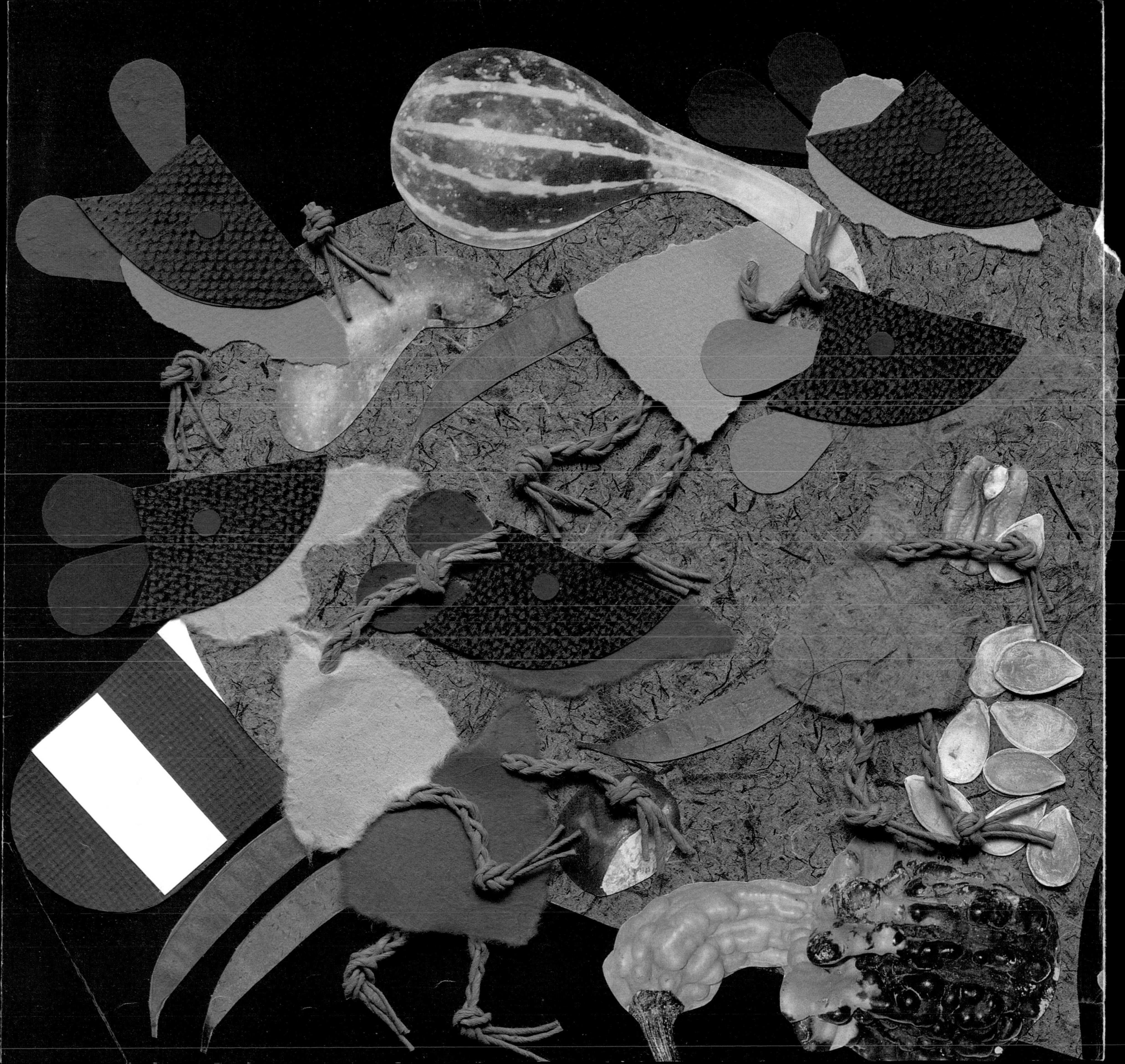

Scat, scary cat.
Have some broccoli!

There's
no mouse
on the menu
at *this* party.

Pumpkin Talk

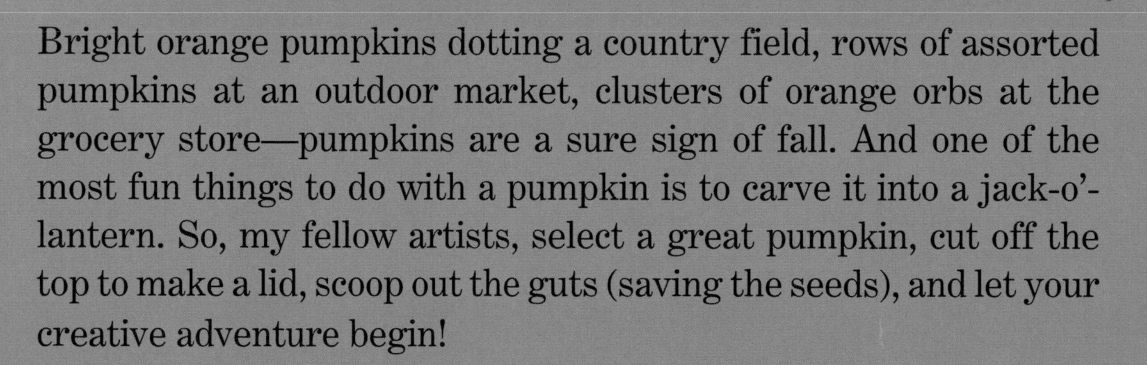

Bright orange pumpkins dotting a country field, rows of assorted pumpkins at an outdoor market, clusters of orange orbs at the grocery store—pumpkins are a sure sign of fall. And one of the most fun things to do with a pumpkin is to carve it into a jack-o'-lantern. So, my fellow artists, select a great pumpkin, cut off the top to make a lid, scoop out the guts (saving the seeds), and let your creative adventure begin!

Roasted pumpkin seeds are delicious. Preheat the oven to 250°. Remove the slimy fiber from the seeds by hand. Spread the seeds in a baking pan. Salt to your taste, then place the pan in the oven. Stir the seeds every fifteen minutes. Repeat until they are brown, crispy, and ready to eat. (And, of course, have an adult help with the cutting and the cooking.)

Harvest Colors
cherry tomato
ornamental gourd
ornamental gourd
ornamental gourds
corn husk
Indian corn
cranberries
strawflower
broom bristles
wheat
carrot
Indian corn
carnival squash

horse chestnuts
black locust seed pods
sycamore fruit
turk's turban squash
pecan
broccoli
elm leaf
crab apples
ornamental gourd
squash seed
pumpkin seed
honey locust seed pod
acorn
fingerling potato
pinecone

For Jane, Maggie, and Jim

Artist Note

The collage illustrations in this book include some of my favorite fall objects, which I photographed, color Xeroxed, and combined with various colored papers, hand-painted papers, handmade papers, Italian marbleized papers, and twine and string.

Acknowledgments

Thanks for photographs from the archives of Pat Tallmadge Ehlert and Dick Ehlert, Jane Ehlert Eickhoff and Rick Eickhoff, and Shirley Ehlert Dinsch and the late Don Dinsch.

BEACH LANE BOOKS
An imprint of Simon & Schuster Children's Publishing Division
1230 Avenue of the Americas, New York, New York 10020

The text for this book is set in Century Expanded.
Manufactured in China
First Edition
10 9 8 7 6 5 4 3 2 1
Library of Congress Cataloging-in-Publication Data
Ehlert, Lois.
Boo to you! / Lois Ehlert. — 1st ed.
p. cm.
Summary: When the neighborhood cat tries to crash the mice's harvest party, they have a plan to scare the intruder away.
ISBN: 978-1-4169-8625-6 (hardcover : alk. paper)
[1. Stories in rhyme. 2. Mice—Fiction. 3. Cats—Fiction. 4. Parties—Fiction.] I. Title.
PZ8.3.E29Bo 2009
[E]—dc22
2008044352